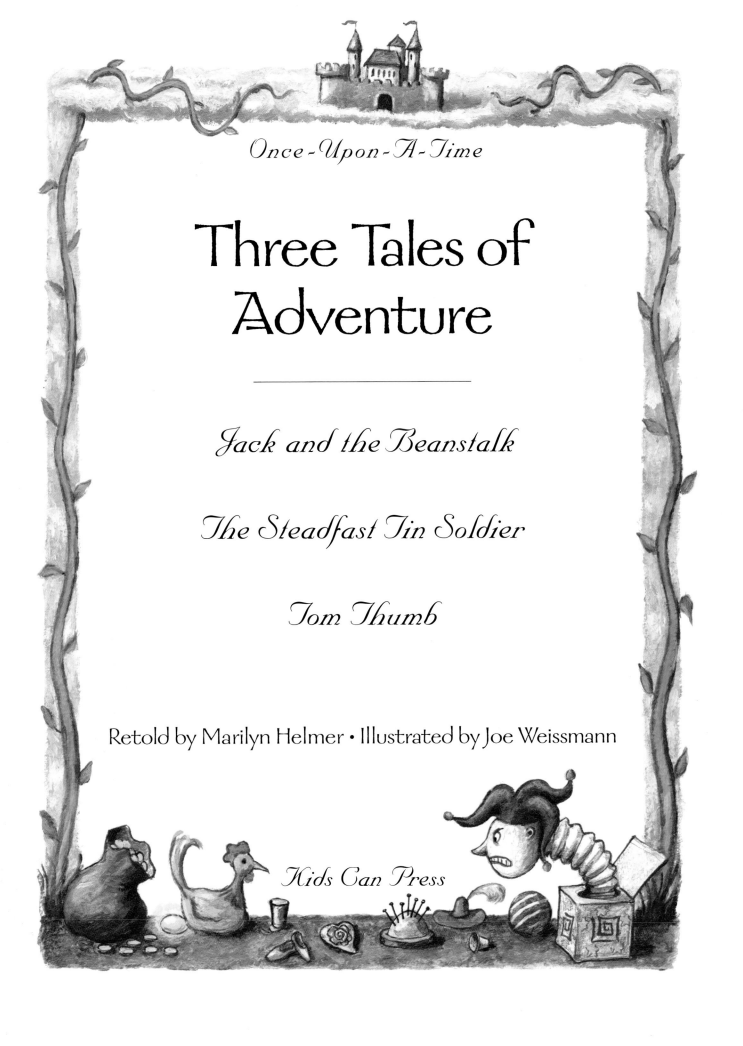

Once-Upon-A-Time

Three Tales of Adventure

Jack and the Beanstalk

The Steadfast Tin Soldier

Tom Thumb

Retold by Marilyn Helmer • Illustrated by Joe Weissmann

Kids Can Press

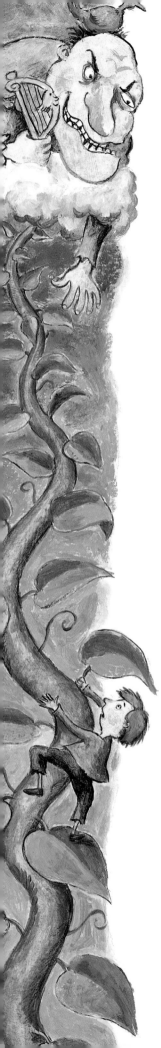

*To David MacDonald, who edited this series with patience,
skill and dedication. I couldn't have done it without you. — M.H.*

*To my wife, Murielle, who puts up with all the strange hours —
with love. — J.W.*

Text © 2004 Marilyn Helmer
Illustrations © 2004 Joe Weissmann

Kids Can Press acknowledges the financial support of the Government of Ontario, through the Ontario Media Development Corporation's Ontario Book Initiative; the Ontario Arts Council; the Canada Council for the Arts; and the Government of Canada, through the BPIDP, for our publishing activity.

Published in Canada by
Kids Can Press Ltd.
29 Birch Avenue
Toronto, ON M4V 1E2

Published in the U.S. by
Kids Can Press Ltd.
2250 Military Road
Tonawanda, NY 14150

www.kidscanpress.com

The artwork in this book was rendered in oils.
The text is set in Berkeley.

Series Editor: Debbie Rogosin
Editor: David MacDonald
Designer: Marie Bartholomew
Printed and bound in Singapore by Tien Wah Press

This book is smyth sewn casebound.

CM 04 0 9 8 7 6 5 4 3 2 1

National Library of Canada Cataloguing in Publication Data

Helmer, Marilyn
        Three tales of adventure / retold by Marilyn Helmer ; illustrated by Joe Weissmann.

(Once-upon-a-time)
Contents: Jack and the beanstalk — The steadfast tin soldier — Tom Thumb.

ISBN 1-55074-945-5

1. Fairy tales. I. Weissmann, Joe, 1947– II. Title. III. Series: Helmer, Marilyn. Once-upon-a-time.

PS8565.E4594T4645 2004   j398.2   C2003-906477-8

Kids Can Press is a ᴸᴼᴿᵁˢ™ Entertainment company

Contents

Jack and the Beanstalk

Once upon a time, a young lad named Jack lived with his mother in a tumbledown farmhouse. They had few possessions other than a black-and-white cow named Bessie. One day Jack's mother went to the cupboard and found it bare. "Our food is all gone," she said. "There's no money to buy more, so we must sell the cow. Take her to market and be sure you get a fair price for her."

So Jack set off with Bessie plodding behind. He hadn't gone far when he met an odd little man who stopped to admire the cow. "I could use a fine animal like her," said the man. "And I will pay you well."

Jack could hardly believe his luck. "How much will you give me?" he asked.

"I will give you something even more valuable than money," said the man. "I'll trade my magic beans for her."

"Magic beans? There's no such thing!" exclaimed Jack.

"Indeed there is," the man said. He opened his hand and showed Jack five brightly colored beans. "Plant these tonight and see what riches they will bring you."

Jack could not resist such a bargain. He grabbed the beans and handed over Bessie's rope. With a whoop and a cheer, he ran home to tell his mother the good news.

To Jack's surprise, his mother was furious. "You traded our Bessie for some worthless beans?" she wailed. "What a fool you are!" She opened the window and flung the beans into the yard. Then she sent Jack to bed without any supper.

The next morning, when Jack looked out the window, an amazing sight greeted him. Beside the house grew an enormous beanstalk, stretching high into the sky.

"I knew those beans were magic!" cried Jack. Quick as a wink he scrambled out the window and onto the beanstalk. Up, up, up he climbed, disappearing into the clouds.

When Jack reached the top, he found himself at the edge of a long, winding road. In the distance stood a towering castle. Jack hurried toward it, wondering what adventures he might find.

By the time he reached the castle, Jack was tired and hungry. He walked up to the huge door and knocked. As it swung open, Jack stared in surprise. Standing in front of him was a woman so tall that he had to bend backward to see her face. She looked down at him from her great height.

"Please, Ma'am," said Jack. "I'm so hungry. Could you give me something to eat?"

"Come in," said the woman. "But you must be careful. My husband is a giant and he has an enormous appetite. If he finds you here, you won't *have* something to eat — you'll *be* something to eat!"

Jack went pale with fear, but his empty stomach gave him courage. "I'll take my chances," he said.

The giant's wife gave him some bread and cheese. Jack had scarcely finished the first bite when he heard a loud *Clump! Bump! Thump!* that shook the castle floor.

"My husband is coming. Quick, hide!" cried the giant's wife, and she pushed Jack into the oven. Jack trembled in the darkness as he heard the giant roar:

Fee, fi, fo, fum,
I smell the blood of an Englishman.
Be he alive or be he dead,
I'll grind his bones to make my bread!

"It's only last night's dinner you smell," Jack heard the giant's wife say. "Come and eat your breakfast, Husband."

Jack peeked through the crack at the edge of the oven door. His eyes widened in amazement as he watched the giant gobble down a breakfast that could have fed ten men.

As soon as the giant had finished eating, he called to his wife, "Bring my sacks of gold!" When the sacks were in front of him, he opened one, spilled the coins onto the table and began to count them: "One... two... three..." Before long, he yawned a giant-sized yawn, put his head on the table and fell fast asleep.

Jack crept out of the oven. He looked about to be sure the giant's wife was nowhere in sight. Then he tiptoed to the table and snatched a sack of gold. He raced to the beanstalk and climbed down as fast as his legs would carry him.

"Mother, come and see what I
have," he cried as he rushed into
the cottage.

When she saw the coins
spread out before her,
Jack's mother could
hardly believe her
eyes. "Bless you, Jack!"
she exclaimed. "There is
enough gold here to last
us for the rest of our lives!"

Now Jack and his mother
were well-off indeed. But Jack was
a restless lad and soon he was ready for
another adventure. Dressed in fine new clothes,
he climbed the beanstalk and headed back to the castle.

Once again Jack knocked on the door. The giant's wife opened it and
peered down at him. "What do you want?" she asked, not recognizing
Jack now that he was dressed like a gentleman.

"Please may I have something to eat?" Jack asked politely.

The giant's wife frowned. "The last time a boy was here, he stole some
of my husband's gold," she declared.

"What an ill-mannered lad!" said Jack with an innocent smile.

He had just managed to tease a bowl of stew from the woman when the
floor began to shake. *Clump! Bump! Thump!* came the sound of heavy feet.
"Mercy, my husband is home!" cried the giant's wife. She pushed Jack into
the broom cupboard. Once again he heard the giant roar:

> *Fee, fi, fo, fum,*
> *I smell the blood of an Englishman.*
> *Be he alive or be he dead,*
> *I'll grind his bones to make my bread!*

His wife quickly spoke up. "Nonsense, it's just the roast pig I cooked for your lunch."

This time, as Jack peeked through a knothole, he saw the giant gulp down a lunch that could have fed twenty men.

The minute he was finished, the giant called out, "Wife, bring my pet hen!" His wife hurried in and set the hen on the table. "Lay, hen, lay!" thundered the giant. Jack watched, astonished, as the hen laid one golden egg, then another, and another!

Jack waited until the giant fell asleep and his wife left the room. Then he sneaked out of the cupboard, grabbed the hen, and ran from the castle as fast as he could. He hurried down the beanstalk and soon he was back home with another treasure to show his mother.

With the gold coins and the hen that laid golden eggs, Jack and his mother could live in luxury for the rest of their lives. But before long, Jack was eager for another adventure. Up the beanstalk and back to the giant's castle he went.

This time Jack sneaked into the castle when the giant's wife wasn't looking. He'd scarcely had time to hide behind the wood bin when *Clump! Bump! Thump!* came the sound of heavy feet and the giant began to roar:

Fee, fi, fo, fum ...

"Goodness, Husband," his wife interrupted, "there isn't another soul here. Come and eat your dinner."

From his hiding place, Jack watched the giant gulp down a dinner that could have fed thirty men.

Then the giant called for his golden harp. The moment his wife placed it before him, he thundered, "Play, harp, play!" A soft lullaby filled the room, and soon the giant's head began to nod.

When Jack was sure the giant was asleep, he tiptoed from behind the wood bin and grabbed the harp. He had almost reached the door when suddenly the harp cried out, "Help me, Master! Help me!"

The giant woke with a furious roar and was after Jack like a hound at the hunt. With the giant close behind, Jack scrambled down the beanstalk. As he neared the bottom he shouted, "Quickly, Mother, bring me the ax!"

The moment Jack's feet touched the ground, his mother handed him the ax. With three mighty blows, Jack chopped through the beanstalk. It teetered and tottered, then over it went, landing with a terrific crash. The giant fell with such force that he was killed on the spot. Jack decided that he'd had enough adventures to last him for many a year to come. With plenty of coins in their pockets, a hen that laid golden eggs, and a harp that played beautiful music, Jack and his mother lived happily for the rest of their lives.

The Steadfast Tin Soldier

Once long ago, a young boy was given a birthday present, neatly wrapped and tied with ribbon. Inside were twenty-five toy soldiers, all made from a single tin spoon.

"Toy soldiers!" cried the boy. "How handsome they are!" And indeed they were, standing straight and tall in their red and blue uniforms. The soldiers were identical, except for the last one, who had only one leg. But that little soldier was so well made that he stood as firmly on one leg as the others did on two. And of the twenty-five, he was to have the greatest adventures of all.

The boy lined up the soldiers, side by side, on a long table. Twenty-four of them looked straight ahead, thinking of nothing but the battles they would fight. The one-legged soldier stood at attention, too, but his eyes took in all the sights. And what a lot there was to see! The playroom was filled with every kind of toy imaginable, but the best of all was a large cardboard castle, complete with turrets. In front was a mirror-glass lake, surrounded by trees. Graceful wax swans seemed to glide across its surface.

But none of this could compare in beauty to the dainty Paper Dancer who stood in front of the castle. She wore a dress of the finest lace, pinned at the shoulder with a sparkling tinsel rose. Balancing on one leg, she held the other high behind her. The Tin Soldier could not see it, and so he believed she, too, had only one leg, just like him.

"She stands every bit as steadfastly as a true soldier," he said to himself. "Wouldn't she be the perfect wife for me! I must find a way to speak to her."

But the more he thought about it, the more he wondered if perhaps she was too grand for him. "I could never ask her to leave her castle and live with me," he said sadly. He hid behind a large jack-in-the-box, where he could look at her without being seen.

Before he went to bed that evening, the boy put the soldiers back into their box. Though he searched high and low, he couldn't find the one-legged soldier, who was still hiding behind the jack-in-the-box.

Soon the house was in darkness and the people were all asleep. Then, as if by magic, the toys woke up. Drums began to drum, flutes tooted and the bears and dolls danced together. Neither the Paper Dancer nor the Tin Soldier joined in. She stood straight and tall as always and he never took his eyes off her, not even for a moment.

Suddenly, as the clock struck midnight, the lid of the jack-in-the-box flew open. Out popped a horrible goblin who glared at the Tin Soldier. "Do not wish for what doesn't belong to you!" he warned.

The Tin Soldier ignored the goblin, and looked only at the beautiful Paper Dancer. The goblin's eyes glittered with rage. "You will be sorry!" he threatened as he disappeared back into the box.

The next day, while the boy was playing, he found the one-legged soldier and moved him to the windowsill. Then a terrible thing happened. It may have been the work of the goblin or perhaps it was just the wind. Somehow the soldier fell out the window and plunged three stories down to the street below!

The boy and his nanny rushed outside to look for him. He was right there, stuck between two cobblestones by the point of his bayonet, but somehow they did not see him. As it began to rain, the Tin Soldier watched them run for cover. He wanted to call out, "Wait! Here I am!" but thought that would be undignified for a man in uniform.

The rain poured down in torrents. Rivers of water rushed along the gutters. Through it all, the Tin Soldier tried to maintain his dignity, even though he was upside down.

When the skies cleared, two street urchins came skipping through the puddles. "Look what I found!" called one. He yanked the soldier out from between the cobblestones.

"Let's send him to sea," said the other. He folded a piece of newspaper into a boat and put the Tin Soldier inside. Then he placed the boat in the gutter.

"What an adventure this will be!" thought the Tin Soldier, for he had never been a ship's captain before. The boat rushed along, swirling and whirling, until the Tin Soldier's face might have turned quite green if it had not been painted pink. Dizzy and frightened though he was, he managed to stand guard at the front of the boat, as steadfast as ever.

Even when the rushing water swept the boat into a deep drain, the Tin Soldier didn't flinch. "Gracious me, where am I going now?" he wondered. "This must be the work of that horrible goblin!" His thoughts turned to the Paper Dancer. "If only we could be together," he sighed.

Now the boat sped on faster than ever. In the distance, the Tin Soldier heard the sound of a roaring waterfall, growing louder and louder. Rounding a bend, he saw daylight ahead. A moment later, toppling and turning, the Tin Soldier and his boat were swept out of the drain and into the canal. The paper boat was torn to pieces and the soldier sank into the depths of the churning water.

All at once, everything went dark. A passing fish, mistaking the soldier for a tasty bug, had swallowed him in one gulp.

"Will my adventures never end?" thought the soldier. "Will I never see my lovely dancer again?" The Tin Soldier's adventures might well have ended there, but the fish was a greedy fellow. He snatched up a delicious-looking green fly, which happened to be on the end of a fisherman's hook.

The fisherman took his catch to market and there, by chance, he sold it to the cook who worked in the very same house where the boy lived. And that is how the Tin Soldier found himself right back where his adventures had begun.

When the cook discovered the Tin Soldier in the fish's belly, she went looking for the boy. She found him in the playroom with his friends. "Look what I have!" she exclaimed, placing the soldier on the table in front of him.

"My soldier!" cried the boy as the children crowded around to see.

How delighted the Tin Soldier was to find himself back in the playroom! Although his paint was chipped and cracked, he stood as straight and tall as ever. Right in front of him stood the Paper Dancer, in her fine lace dress with the tinsel rose twinkling at her shoulder. "Why, she has never moved at all," thought the soldier. "She has stood in front of her castle, steadfast and true."

Now it may have been the work of the wicked goblin or perhaps it was just a childish prank. But all of a sudden, for no reason, one of the boys snatched up the Tin Soldier and threw him into the fire!

As the flames danced around him, the little Tin Solder stood as steadfast as ever. His eyes were on the Paper Dancer and, to his great joy, he saw that she was gazing fondly at him.

Then a wonderful thing happened. Whether it was the wind or the magic of love, the Paper Dancer suddenly left her castle. She whirled gracefully through the air, right into the arms of the Tin Soldier.

The next morning, as the maid swept the ashes from the fireplace, she came across a strange metal object, which she gave to the boy.

The object was covered with ash. When the boy gently cleaned it off, he found a piece of tin melted into the shape of a heart. In the middle was the tinsel rose. The boy kept the heart and one day, when he became a soldier himself, he gave it to a girl who looked a lot like the little Paper Dancer.

Tom Thumb

Once upon a time there was a woodsman and his wife who had no children of their own. "If only we had a little one, we would not be so lonely," said the woodsman.

"A child would make my happiness complete," said the wife, "even if he were no bigger than my thumb."

In time, just as the woman had hoped, she gave birth to a baby boy, and indeed he was no bigger than her thumb. The couple was thrilled. "My fondest wish has come true," the wife rejoiced.

"Let us call him Tom Thumb," said the husband, and so they did.

As the years passed, Tom grew more handsome and clever, but he never grew one bit bigger. Despite his small size, he was quite helpful to his parents. He picked the wild strawberries no one else could find and searched for eggs the hens hid in the grass. He even helped drive the cows to the meadow, using a straw as a tiny whip.

One day Tom's father was going to the forest to cut wood. "I wish I had someone to bring the horse and cart to me at the end of the day," he said.

"I can do it!" Tom offered. "If Mother puts me in the horse's ear, I'll whisper directions to guide him." When the time came, with a "Gee-up" and a "Whoa," Tom brought the horse and cart right to where his father was working.

If Tom wasn't busy helping his parents, there was nothing he liked better than a good adventure. One day he played hide-and-seek in the hay and almost became the cow's lunch. Another time he went for a swim in the milk pail and was nearly churned into butter. But these were small adventures compared to the one that began the day he fell into the plum-pudding batter.

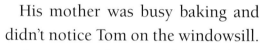

His mother was busy baking and didn't notice Tom on the windowsill. He was peeking out from behind the curtain, curious to see what she was making. When she went to the pantry to get the plums, Tom jumped down and scrambled up the side of the bowl. As he looked over the edge, suddenly— *plop!* — he tumbled into the batter and sank right to the bottom.

With his mouth full of pudding batter, Tom couldn't call for help. His mother stirred in the plums and poured the whole thing into a pan. She popped it straight into the oven with Tom in the middle!

The batter got hotter and hotter, and so did poor Tom. "Ow! Ow! Ouch!" he cried as he frantically hopped about. *Cling! Clang! Clatter*! The pan slid this way and that, banging against the sides of the oven.

"That pudding is bewitched!" cried Tom's mother. She snatched the tin from the oven and tossed it out the window.

The pudding landed right at the feet of a tinker who was passing by. "Oh, lucky day!" he cried. "What a delicious dinner this will make." But as he picked it up, he heard the pudding shout, "Let me out! Let me out!"

"A talking pudding!" cried the terrified tinker. "I want no part of that!" He threw the tin over his shoulder and dashed off down the road.

Tom wiggled and squirmed and finally pushed his way out of the pudding. There he stood at the edge of the road, covered in crumbs and sticky batter.

All might have been well if, at that very moment, a hungry raven hadn't flown by. Thinking that Tom was just the right size for lunch, the raven snatched him up and carried him off before you could say *plum pudding!*

This did not suit Tom at all. He jerked and kicked until the raven decided that her lunch was just a bit too lively. She let go of Tom, and down, down, down he dropped, into the lake below.

A large fish, looking for a handy meal, saw Tom splash into the water. With a snap and a gulp, the fish swallowed Tom whole. Now you might think that Tom's adventures had come to a sad end, but it wasn't so. The fish that had just caught Tom suddenly found itself tangled in a fisherman's net.

"What a fine catch this is!" exclaimed the fisherman. "Fine enough for the King himself. I'll give it to His Highness as a gift, for there's nothing he enjoys more than a meal of freshly caught fish." And that is how Tom ended up on the royal dinner table.

Imagine the surprise of the King and Queen when Tom stepped out of the fish's mouth. What a tale he had to tell!

Everyone in the court was delighted with the tiny boy and his big adventures. "If you stay with us, I shall have a gold palace built, just the right size for you," said the King.

"I would be happy to live here," Tom agreed, thrilled with the idea of his very own palace.

The King ordered the royal tailor to sew Tom a wardrobe of fine clothes, and the silversmith crafted a miniature suit of armor to match the King's own. With a trained mouse to ride on and a darning needle for his sword, Tom made a splendid little knight. Banquets were given in his honor and people came from near and far to hear of his wonderful adventures.

The Queen watched all this with jealous eyes. "I was the darling of the court before this miserable wisp of a lad came along," she muttered. "There must be a way to get rid of him." So one day she whispered to the King, "Have you noticed that Tom seems rather glum lately? Perhaps the dear boy is homesick. I think we should send him back to his parents." The King agreed reluctantly, for he was sad to see Tom go.

When Tom arrived home, his parents greeted him with shouts of joy. They had missed him sorely and wondered whatever had become of him.

It was not long before everyone at the palace began to miss Tom, too. Even the Queen admitted that life seemed dull without the tiny boy and his wonderful stories. Soon after, the King went to visit Tom and asked him to come back and live at the palace. To Tom's parents he said, "I will build you a cottage close by so that you may see your son any time you wish."

Tom was only too happy to return, for he had missed the fun and excitement of the court. There he lived for the rest of his life, having many more adventures and entertaining everyone he met with his delightful tales.

Success and adventure will surely come
If you're as clever and brave as tiny Tom Thumb!